Gangs of Brighton

Paul Blum

RISING STARS

NASEN House, 4/5 Amber Business Village, Amber Close,
Amington, Tamworth, Staffordshire, B77 4RP

Rising Stars UK Ltd.
7 Hatchers Mews, Bermondsey Street, London SE1 3GS
www.risingstars-uk.com

Text and design © Rising Stars UK Ltd.
The right of Paul Blum to be identified as the author of this
work has been asserted by him in accordance with the
Copyright, Design and Patents Act, 1988.

Published 2012

Cover design: Burville-Riley Partnership
Brighton photographs: iStock
Illustrations: Chris King for Illustration Ltd (characters and cover artwork)/
Abigail Daker (map) http://illustratedmaps.info
Text design and typesetting: Geoff Rayner
Publisher: Rebecca Law
Editorial manager: Sasha Morton Creative Project Management

British Library Cataloguing in Publication Data.
A CIP record for this book is available from the British Library.

ISBN: 978-0-85769-600-7

Printed and bound by CPI Group (UK) Ltd, Croydon, CR0 4YY

Contents

Name:
John Logan

Age:
24

Hometown:
Manchester

Occupation:
Author of
supernatural
thrillers

Special skills:
Not yet known

Name:
Rose Petal

Age:
22

Hometown:
Brighton

Occupation:
Yoga teacher,
nightclub and
shop owner,
vampire hunter

Special skills:
Private investigator
specialising in
supernatural
crime

Location map

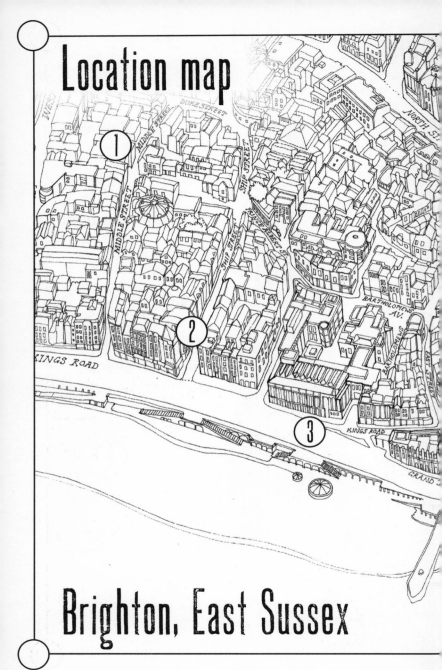

Brighton, East Sussex

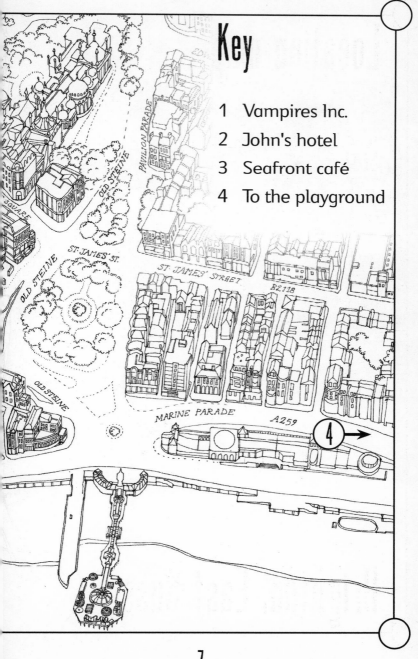

Key

1 Vampires Inc.
2 John's hotel
3 Seafront café
4 To the playground

Chapter 1

The gang pulled up on their large motorbikes in front of a café by the sea. Their engines drowned out the sound of the waves. A group of tourists sitting in the café looked up at the noise. When they saw the bikers they were frightened. They grabbed their coats and bags, and ran.

The café owner tried to get indoors, but the bikers surrounded him. He reached for his mobile phone to call the police but they were too fast for him. Throwing the phone onto the pebbly beach and smashing it, they seemed to grow before his very eyes. They became taller, stronger and even more deadly.

'Tell the band of vampires we'll see them on Saturday,' said the gang leader from the seat of his bike. He revved the engine and snarled at the elderly man. 'We know he's coming. He knows this is our turf. You get the message to him. Tell him it will be all of our boys and all of his!'

The rest of the gang jumped back onto their bikes and revved them up. Even the bikes seemed to have grown bigger. The machines looked like angry cats, showing their teeth, snarling and hissing. Their riders' eyes became red. Their faces changed. They looked like a pack of wolves. Big, hungry wolves.

Just then, police sirens started to wail

nearby. The elderly café owner looked around and when he looked back, the bikers had gone. He knew what he had to do.

****

Four days earlier ...
Rose Petal was having a good night out. She had taken her best friend Mina to a gig in London. They both loved the band The Night Killers. Their lead singer was called Alex Reddy and Mina thought he was really cute.

'But he's a mod, not a goth,' said Rose Petal. 'He's not really one of us.' Rose and Mina both dyed their hair, wore black clothes and had lots of tattoos and piercings. Mina taught

Rose's yoga classes when she was busy and sometimes worked at Vampires Inc., Rose's nightclub.

'Mods can be cool,' said Mina. 'I love the way they whizz around on those shiny scooters with all the mirrors.'

'They do seem to like vampire culture,' said Rose. 'They spend a lot of money in my shop on candles and herbs, and they like hanging out in the club.'

'Don't you fancy any of them?' asked Mina.

'Of course not!' said Rose. But she blushed a little as she said it. She didn't tell Mina that Alex Reddy kept staring at her from the stage.

After the gig, Alex pushed his way

through the crowd to Mina and Rose. 'You were great,' said Mina, trying to get Alex's attention.

'Thanks. But what did you think?' said Alex, looking at Rose with his deep brown eyes. She nodded. 'It was really good. Maybe you could play at my club in Brighton some time? It's called Vampires Inc., but it's a bit smaller than this place!'

'If it means I get to see you again we'll play anywhere,' he said to Rose with a grin. He carried on talking to her and turned his back on Mina. After a few minutes, Mina stomped off to the bar in a bad mood.

'That was rude,' said Rose. She went to walk away but Alex took her arm and made her look up at him. Something in his eyes stopped her from leaving.

'I'm sorry, Rose, I will apologise to your friend. I just really want to get to know you, not her. And yes, the band can play at your club whenever you like. How about this weekend?' Alex really was charming, so Rose decided not to try to find Mina just yet.

'It's a bank holiday this weekend so the club will be rammed. You'll probably get mobbed, but it would be great to see you again. I mean, have the band play there.' Rose blushed. What was wrong with her? She was acting like an overgrown schoolgirl!

Alex smiled and leaned down to

whisper in her ear, 'Saturday's a date. I'll ring you to sort out the details.' Then he was gone.

Mina came back over and grumbled, 'He may be cute, but he's got bad manners.'

'Hmm,' said Rose. 'He's okay, actually. Give him a chance.'

But as they were leaving, Rose realised something strange. She hadn't told Alex her name. So how did he know who she was?

Chapter 2

Late on Saturday afternoon, Rose and Alex Reddy were at Vampires Inc., sitting on the edge of the small stage. Rose was laughing as Alex asked her lots of questions about her and her life in Brighton. In the corner of the club, John Logan sat at his laptop, trying to make sense of some of Rose's research notes. She was helping John to understand the dark side of the city, where vampires, ghosts and other supernatural creatures existed alongside humans.

John was going to write a second book about the supernatural, but today

he was having trouble concentrating.
There was something about Alex that
he didn't like. Rose was clearly a big fan
of his, though. John had never heard
her talk so much. They even looked
alike in their black clothes and with
their matching shoulder tattoos. Rose's
was a tiger and Alex's was a bat in
flight. John didn't like Alex or his tattoo.

'So, I'm trying to make enough
money out of Vampires Inc. to go back
to university,' he heard Rose say.

'What will you study?' asked Alex.
Rose felt the full force of his attention.
He gave off a lot of energy. He made
her feel as if she was the only person in
the whole world.

'Folklore and the history of the

supernatural,' she replied. John was surprised. He thought she was already an expert on that stuff. Maybe he should ask Rose about her life a bit more too.

Rose saw Alex smile in the candlelight. 'Does that mean vampires, witches, werewolves, that kind of thing? I wouldn't mess with those kinds of worlds,' he said in a low voice. 'They can be dangerous.'

A darkness came over his face as he spoke. For a second, he was like a stranger.

'I know,' she said softly. 'The world of the supernatural is closer to the human world than most people want to believe.'

'Just promise me you'll be careful, Rose ...' he started to say, taking her hand. Just then, John called over to them.

'Rose, any chance we can get some lights on in here? It's pitch-black and your handwriting is hard enough to read in broad daylight.'

Rose glared at John. Alex glared at John. John glared at both of them. Then Alex jumped down from the stage and gave Rose a kiss on the cheek. 'I need to get some sleep before the show. See you later, pretty lady.' With that, he pulled on his long, dark coat and left through the back door of the club.

'See you later, Alex,' called John.

Rose snapped on the main lights and stormed up the stairs without saying a word to him. 'Thanks!' he muttered, going back to Rose's notes. But for some reason, he still couldn't concentrate.

Chapter 3

That night, Vampires Inc. was packed.
The Night Killers were a big band
and their fans had filled the club.
They were singing along to the band's
songs at top volume. Danny, the white
owl, was sitting on his special perch
looking at the crowds around him. His
green eyes were watching everyone
and everything. Mina served drinks as
quickly as she could, but John had never
seen so many people in such a small
space. Strangely, Rose was nowhere to
be seen.

Rose kept telling John: 'Knowledge

is power. My customers know the vampire community better than anyone else.' So John was on research duty at Vampires Inc., trying to get to know the clients. He waved to Rodney, who he knew was half werewolf. Rodney was also a fortune-teller who loved to dance and Rose adored him.

Just then, a vampire girl Logan had met in the club before came up to him. 'Hey John, has Rose left you all on your own?' giggled Hazel. 'Come and dance with me!'

Logan found himself being dragged onto the dance floor. He bumped into a group of girls who were screaming Alex Reddy's name. As John tried to move away from Hazel, he saw Rose's red hair. It was lit up by one of the stage spotlights. She was at the front of the crowd, staring up at Alex as if she had been hypnotised.

Suddenly, he saw Rodney stop dancing and freeze on the spot. The hairs on Rodney's arms and neck seemed to stand on end. Then a blinding pain shot through John's head. He staggered back as he heard Rodney's voice in his mind.

'Clear the club, get Rose to safety. Danger is on the way,' said Rodney's voice in his head. 'Trouble is coming on four legs. Hurry, John!'

John Logan looked out of the dark windows of the club. Across the street, he saw several large motorbikes pull up. The music covered up the roar of their engines. Logan looked back at the stage to see the elderly café owner pass a piece of paper to the drummer. Within seconds, the song ended. Alex shouted into the microphone, 'We are The Night Killers. Goodnight!'

The stage lights went black and the band disappeared. The crowd groaned, then started shouting and clapping for more. John pushed his way through the customers and jumped over the bar. He flicked on the main lights and started shouting, 'Show's over, everyone out! Bar's closed!'

Rose was suddenly by his side, looking dazed. 'John, what are you doing? What's going on?' John dragged her to the window and pointed at the motorbike gang who were taking off their helmets.

'Do you know them?' John asked.

'I know of them,' she said. 'They're the Lukos Chapter. "Lukos" is the Greek word for wolf. They usually hang out way past the West Pier, but every so often they come into town to pick a fight.'

The club's customers carried on drinking and calling for the band. They didn't hear the thud of biker boots or see the bikers push their way in without buying a ticket. The gang's leader elbowed his way to the bar and swept everything off the counter. He grabbed a glass and flung it across the room. Everybody started screaming. Some of the customers ran for the stairs. Others tried to get down on the floor.

The five members of the Lukos Chapter started to knock over the tables and chairs. Danny, Rose's white owl, bravely dived on them but they slapped him away.

The bikers seemed to grow as they smashed up the club. Their arms and shoulders got bigger. Their hair got longer. Their eyes gleamed red. Rodney tried to speak to them, but they pushed him to the ground. John saw Hazel try to run away, but she slipped on the wet floor and fell against a snapped chair leg. The broken wood went through her chest and she exploded in a pile of grey ash.

Rose and John dashed for the stage exit. On their way, John saw a single silver drumstick lying on the floor. Its end was shaped into a sharp point. Thinking it might be useful, he put it in his jeans pocket before slamming through the fire exit.

The band's black van had gone. Alex's mirrored scooter was just visible at the end of the street. As they watched, it seemed to sparkle and glow. Then it melted into a smooth silver shape that grew wings and lifted off into the sky.

'Woah!' gasped John. Suddenly, he knew what was going on. 'Rose, I think your boyfriend is a vampire.'

Chapter 4

Soon, the noise inside the club died down. John and Rose crept back inside and heard the gang rev up their bikes and kick off. They also heard them howl like wolves at the moon.

John looked around the empty room. Rodney and Mina's heads peeked up from behind the bar. 'Don't worry about the mess, Rose, we'll sort it out,' said Rodney. Mina was crying and Rose looked shocked and pale.

'Thanks for the tip-off,' said John quietly to Rodney. Rodney smiled and handed John a piece of paper. 'Give this to Rose. She needs to stop the fight.'

Vampires:
the Lukos Chapter
will meet you at the
playground at midnight.

All of you.
All of us.
Kill or be killed.

Now Logan could understand why he had taken such a dislike to Alex Reddy. Rose had invited a gang of vampires into town by mistake. Vampires who were at war with the local werewolves. Brilliant.

John showed Rose the note and quickly explained what was going on. 'We've got to stop the fight,' he said.

She nodded. 'I know. It's far more dangerous than it seems. When they fight each other they'll be in their vampire and werewolf forms. They must have an old score to settle. Tonight is a full moon. The werewolves will be at their most powerful and I don't want Alex to get hurt.'

'Hurt?' shouted John. 'I know I'm not

an expert, but I think having a vampire boyfriend might be a bad idea for a vampire hunter! You have to keep the people of Brighton safe. Hazel's dead! No one else can get caught up in this mess!'

'I know,' cried Rose. 'This is my mess. I really need your help to sort it out.'

****

Four miles outside Brighton, a path ran under the white cliff by the sea. Once the site of an open-air swimming pool, now there was a wide playground there. It was here that the vampires and werewolves took their fight. Rose directed John in his hired car. Soon they were hiding at the top of the cliff and looking down onto the battle.

John learned more about vampires and werewolves by watching the fight than from anything else. It was a terrifying sight. He was shaking all over and Rose gripped his arm in fear.

Both gangs fought with all of their strength. Evil radiated from the vampires as they drank the blood of the wolves they caught. John saw the drummer from the band being pinned down and then heard a horrible shriek. Rose screamed 'No!' and started heading down to the battle.

Running after her, John saw that one of the werewolves had trapped Alex. Shouting at Rose to stop, John couldn't reach her in time. She threw herself between the werewolf and the vampire. They both froze. Then Alex tried to push her aside and the werewolf leapt at Rose.

Without thinking, John grabbed the silver drumstick from his back pocket. He thrust it like a dagger deep into the side of the werewolf as it flew past him. There was a long, high-pitched howl, then silence. The battle stopped. On the ground, a young man lay where the wolf had been. He wasn't breathing. Silver was deadly for werewolves and John had killed one of them with the drumstick. John started to sob as he knelt by the body. What had he done?

****

Rose drove John back to her flat. She made him a mug of herbal tea while Danny, the white owl, sat on his arm.

'I have never seen anything so terrible,' he said. 'Not even in my worst nightmares. How many were killed? What happened to Alex?'

'It isn't easy for vampires and werewolves to kill each other. What you saw doesn't happen often. They lost three men each. They've called a truce. Alex has gone back to London. Turns out he's one of the Elders, who are the oldest vampire coven in Europe. He's very powerful, and could be useful to us in the future. He won't hurt anyone. And don't worry about any more trouble from our furry friends. I think the wolves will go into hiding for a while now. I had a word with their leader.'

Rose took Logan's hand again. 'You should stay on the sofa tonight. You can't drive to your hotel like this.'

John nodded. He felt too weak to move. 'Humans must never get to see such awful things,' he said. 'I can't believe I killed someone, Rose.'

Rose sighed. 'It was kill or be killed. Those are the rules. They'll move on and so will you.' She squeezed his hand.

John couldn't sleep that night. He heard Rose crying in her room, and realised she had really liked Alex Reddy. Maybe the singing vampire would come back to her one day. The thought made John feel weird. He lay awake until dawn and tried to work out what that meant. By morning, he still didn't know.

Glossary

mobbed – surrounded by fans

packed – when a place is full of people

revved – when the engine of a motorbike is given more power, so it can go faster

siren(s) – the noise a police car makes when it is going to an emergency

snarled – growled angrily

supernatural – life that is not human such as ghosts, vampires and werewolves

surrounded – a person finds that there are people all around them and they cannot get away

tip-off – secret information given by one person to another

Quiz

1   What is the name of Alex Reddy's rock band?

2   Who becomes Alex Reddy's girlfriend?

3   Who starts to get jealous of this new relationship?

4   Who warns John Logan that the club is about to be attacked?

5   How do The Night Killers know the werewolves have arrived?

6   Where do the vampires and werewolves fight each other?

7   Why are the werewolves especially strong that night?

8   Who saves Rose's life in the fight?

9   What does Rose give John to help him relax after the fight?

10 How many vampires and werewolves are killed in the battle?

Quiz answers

1   The Night Killers

2   Rose Petal

3   John Logan

4   Rodney

5   The elderly café owner passes the band's drummer a note

6   At a playground under the cliffs

7   It is a full moon

8   John Logan

9   Herbal tea

10 Three vampires and three werewolves

About the author

The author of these books teaches in a London school. At the weekend, his research takes him to the beaches and back streets of Brighton in search of werewolves and vampires.

He writes about what he has found.

Hunter's Moon

Ace of Spades

Face Lift

Vampire Child

Gangs of Brighton

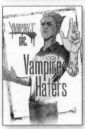
Vampire Haters

End Game

Life is Forever

The Vampires Inc. books are available now
at your local bookshop or from
www.risingstars-uk.com

RISING STARS

Freephone 0800 091 1602 for more information